FAMILY MATTERS!

STEP BY STEP

KV-381-275

Written by Cathy Cassidy

Illustrated by Alan Brown

OXFORD
UNIVERSITY PRESS

Words to look out for ...

caution (*noun*)
Caution is care that you take to avoid a risk, difficulty or mistakes.

classify (*verb*)
classifies, classifying, classified
To classify someone or something is to say what kind of person or thing they are, or which group they belong to.

defer (*verb*)
defers, deferring, deferred
1. To defer something is to put it off until later.
2. To defer to someone is to give way to their wishes or authority.

distinctive (*adjective*)
clearly different from others, and easy to recognize or notice

intervene (*verb*)
intervenes, intervening, intervened
to interrupt what is being said or done in order to stop it or affect the result

integral (*adjective*)
an essential part of something

rational (*adjective*)
reasonable or sensible

recur (*verb*)
recurs, recurring, recurred
Something recurs when it happens again.

unaware (*adjective*)
If you are unaware of something, you do not know about it.

unpredictable (*adjective*)
Something is unpredictable when it is not possible to know what will happen before it actually happens.

Introducing ...

MELODY
(story narrator)

STEFANO
(Melody's dad and
Sylvie's boyfriend)

SYLVIE
(Stefano's girlfriend
and Dino's mum)

DINO
(Sylvie's son)

NINA
(a girl in Dino and Melody's class)

Chapter 1

It's the end of the world as I know it. Well, it might as well be. Every single thing I know and love has been taken away from me. Now I'm stuck in the back of Dad's car as he drives us away from home to the Land That Time Forgot.

I am wedged between our suitcases and boxes of belongings, and I've been frowning hard the whole journey because I really, really don't want to cry.

'You like Sylvie, don't you?' Dad keeps on saying. 'I know we can make this work, Melody!'

I seriously doubt it. I have met Sylvie Owusu, Dad's girlfriend of eight months, just a handful of times.

OK, she seems nice, but that doesn't mean I want my dad to *marry* her. It definitely doesn't mean I want her as a stepmum.

A stepfamily? No thanks.

'I feel bad that you haven't even met Dino yet,' Dad says, as we pass a signpost for Thornton-on-Sea. 'I tried to get us all together a few times. It just hasn't worked out ...'

It hasn't worked out because I invented a few after-school classes to get me out of the meetings, but Dad doesn't know that. I didn't know we'd end up moving in with them, did I?

'You'll like Dino,' Dad says. 'He's about your age. You'll have lots in common!'

'I doubt it,' I mutter. 'Why didn't you tell me sooner, Dad? It's one thing to get engaged to Sylvie, but moving us into her house? It's kind of major!'

'It is, I know,' Dad admits. 'I should have talked to you earlier about proposing to Sylvie, but I wasn't sure she'd say yes. But she did, and so the next <u>rational</u> step was for us all to live together. I thought it'd be a nice surprise for you!'

A nice surprise? That would be a trip to Paris, a new pair of trainers or even a pet rabbit. Not moving to Thornton-on-Sea and a stepbrother I've never met.

<u>Rational</u> means reasonable or sensible.

Thornton-on-Sea is a seaside town stuck in some kind of time-warp. I looked it up on the internet. It has a <u>distinctive</u> old-fashioned pier and not much else at all. You might have fun there on a summer's day, but live there? No thanks.

I'm furious with Dad, but he's terrible at talking about personal stuff. He has been ever since Mum died. The light went out of his eyes, and he seemed to shut down. He didn't talk about why we suddenly had to stop shopping in the expensive stores. He didn't explain why I had to leave my posh school or why we had to sell our flat, but I worked it out. We were short of money, even if Dad couldn't bring himself to say it.

I understood though. He was sad. I was sad, too. Sometimes it was the kind of sad that meant you didn't even want to get up and eat your croissant every morning, but we muddled along together anyway.

<u>Distinctive</u> means clearly different from others, and easy to recognize or notice.

Then Dad went to some comedy night and met Sylvie, who was performing. He offered to manage her and, before long, they started dating. I didn't mind at first. Then again, I didn't know it would end up like *this*.

'This move will be so good for us,' Dad is saying. 'Family life in a nice, ordinary town and no more *celebrity this* or *celebrity that* ...'

'You must be joking!' I growl.

But Dad is serious. He is engaged to Sylvie. That means they'll get married. Sylvie will be my stepmum and some kid called Dino will be my stepbrother. We'll all live happily ever after in Dumpsville-on-Sea.

We turn into a narrow street, and Dad stops the car beside a small red-brick terraced house. I get out and drag my suitcase onto the pavement. Sylvie appears, her face shining with happiness. She throws her arms out wide to welcome us.

I spot the diamond engagement ring on her finger. Broke or not, Dad can still buy a fancy ring for his fiancée.

'You're here!' Sylvie is saying, beaming.

'Come in! You're so welcome, Melody,' she continues. And of course, you need to meet Dino!'

I go inside.

A tall boy with thick curly hair is sitting on the stairs, blinking at me with the same kind of shocked look I must be wearing. I try for a smile, but it comes out more like a scowl. Sylvie is waffling on about the bedroom she's prepared and how I should make myself at home. A wave of anger rolls over me, because this isn't home. It never will be.

'Meet Dino? I don't think so,' I mutter.

I need to get away from these people.

I curl my lip and push past Dino, stomping up the stairs. I find the little room with box-fresh pink bedding and slam the door behind me. Only then do I let myself fall apart.

Tears spill out and rain down my cheeks.

The only person I want right now is Mum. She knew how to hold me tight and whisper exactly the right things to make me feel better. She always understood, but she can't help me now. Nobody can.

My mum was sweet and funny and actually, properly famous. Her name was Melanie Morris.

Most people have heard of her. She was runner-up on a reality TV show called *Housemates*, before I was born.

Dad was her agent, which meant that after the show he got her loads more work on TV and in magazines. They got married and I was born. Everyone loved Mum ... me and Dad most of all.

Money was no problem back then. Our flat looked out over the river. We went on trips to places like Milan, where Dad grew up, and New York ... we were happy.

Then it all went wrong. Mum got really ill

and was in and out of hospital for months.
She passed away two years ago. I don't like
to talk about it because it hurts so much.
I cried every night for months and months.
I still do, sometimes.

When I was little, I had the best family
in the world. Mum even helped me start
my own online channel making videos.
She appeared in the first few with me, so
lots of people watched them. These days
I am probably one of the youngest online
influencers around. Companies send me
things for free to review – books, clothes,
toys ... stuff like that. The kind of things
a ten-year-old girl might like.

I've got loads of followers.

And they're all completely <u>unaware</u> of
how my life is falling apart. I didn't think it
could get any worse, but guess what?

It could. I bury my face in the pillow and
cry and cry and cry.

If you are <u>unaware</u> of something, you do not know
about it.

13

Chapter 2

I wake late, my eyes sore from crying. For a moment I don't know where I am. I don't recognize the little bedroom with the pink bedding and fluffy blanket. Then I realize. My new bedroom, in Thornton-on-Sea.

Last night, Dad came in and tried to get me to go downstairs. 'Come on,' he said. 'I've made a special meal for us all, to celebrate. It's Sylvie's birthday ... and our first day as a family together, too!'

As if I want to celebrate.

Later Dad brought me up a plate of his signature risotto and a glass of juice. He was wearing a cardboard party hat that kept slipping off his head.

I get up and sneak into the bathroom to shower away the sadness. I pull on leggings and one of my favourite jumpers, then check my channel.

My last post was a few days back, before everything went wrong.

'The show must go on,' Mum used to say, back when she had a TV show to do but wasn't in the mood for it. 'Fake it till you make it!'

'Fake it?' I remember asking. Mum explained that acting happy sometimes helped you to feel that way for real. She'd switch on a dazzling smile. Nobody would ever have guessed she wasn't loving every minute! It's one thing I learned well from her.

I unpack my little phone tripod and halo lamp, then take a package out of my suitcase. Inside is a cute fluffy hat with fake animal ears. I talk about the stuff companies send me on my channel. If my followers like something, they go out and buy it.

It's a kind of advertising, really.

I adjust the hat and check the mirror to ensure there's no sign of last night's tears. Then I put my phone into the tripod and press record.

'Hey everyone, Melody here! It may be almost spring, but the weather is still <u>unpredictable</u>! So I'm keeping warm with this lovely hat from Harley's Hats! It's super-soft and super-cute, a total bargain too ... so get saving that pocket money! We all need a fun hat, right? Animal ears just make the world a better place ...'

I grin brightly, leaning closer to the phone camera. 'What else is going on? Oh, SO much! I can't say any more right now, but I'll tell you next time, I promise. Life for Melody Morris is never dull! I'm off to see if my local Harley's Hats have these in other colours, too ... I might see you there! Don't forget to like and comment and tell me what you think!'

If something is <u>unpredictable</u>, it is not possible to know what will happen.

I click off the halo light, my energy fading along with it.

I quickly ditch the hat and the smile slides off my face. The house has fallen very quiet. I wonder if everyone has gone out? I hope so.

I tiptoe down the stairs to the kitchen. A faint smell of coffee and toast tells me I've missed breakfast, so I open a cupboard in search of croissants.

'Everything OK? The lovebirds have gone for a quick walk along the seafront ...'

I almost jump out of my skin to find Dino is behind me, smiling, wearing an old jumper and ancient furry slippers. I want to tell him to go away and leave me alone. Then I remember that this is his house and his kitchen.

I'm the one who doesn't belong here.

'They were holding hands,' he comments.

'Yuck!' I say.

Dino shrugs. 'I know. Although Mum hasn't looked so happy in ages.'

'Dad's had a rough few years, too,' I admit. 'I'm happy for them, but ... it's still a shock.'

'I know,' Dino says.

I ask about croissants, but he hasn't even heard of them.

'Never mind,' I say, shaking cornflakes into a bowl. 'You probably don't get them in Thornton-on-Sea.'

At this, Dino launches into a long speech. He insists this place isn't as bad as I think, and that we should try to make the best of things. Dad and Sylvie are going to get married, whether we like it or not.

'I don't like it,' I say, just in case there's any doubt. 'Your mum's nice, and I've nothing against you either, but I just don't really want a stepfamily.'

'Me neither,' Dino says. He gives a quick

20

grin. 'It's like … a step too far!'

It's not a very funny play on words, but I try for a smile. 'I know … we're … out of step!' I say back.

Dino laughs. 'At least we agree on that.' Then he sighs. 'We're not calling the shots here, are we?'

We're really not. I start telling him about my old life and, without warning, a big tear slides down my cheek. I can't believe it. I don't cry in front of anyone. Not ever.

Dino offers me a tissue, and I blot my eyes furiously.

'It'll be OK,' Dino says. This is such a ridiculous statement. I find myself telling him all the reasons why it won't be, can't be. I tell him about my mum and how everything has crumbled away since she died. He looks suitably shocked and sad.

I haven't talked like this to anyone before. To begin with, it was just too hard.

When I first changed schools, I tried to put on a brave face. 'The show must go on,' as Mum would have said.

But Dino has seen me cry now, and we seem to have bonded over a tissue and some cornflakes.

Then I tell him about being an influencer and show him today's video. It already has more than 700 'likes'. I'm not sure he gets what a big deal this is. He starts telling me that he likes making sci-fi videos, which is clearly not the same thing at all.

'D'you like hot chocolate?' he asks, and I laugh because seriously, who doesn't? 'I made some chocolate chip cookies, too, for Mum's birthday.'

He arranges wonky biscuits on a plate. I take the least weird-looking one. It actually tastes good.

'Thornton-on-Sea is OK,' he insists, trying to cheer me up. 'I would classify it as ordinary, but it's still OK.'

I smile. 'Dino, don't you get it? I don't *do* ordinary!'

He shrugs. 'So ... rise above it!'

'Rise above it?' I echo. 'You mean ... like ... find the sparkle?'

'Sure,' he says. 'Whatever.'

I'm grinning now, a new idea forming. 'That's just the angle I need for my channel. *Find the sparkle! Rise above the ordinary!* Dino, that's a really cool idea!'

To classify someone or something is to say what kind of person or thing they are, or which group they belong to.

23

I pocket my mobile, and pick up the hot chocolate and the cookie. Then I race upstairs to work out how I can use this for my channel. I don't do ordinary, but I can rise above it.

I can do *extra*ordinary.

I can do that really well.

Chapter 3

Starting a new school is no big deal, or that's what I tell myself. Fake it till you make it, right? I'll try my best.

It didn't really work the last time I had to switch schools. The other kids thought I was showing off. I suppose I was a bit, but only because I wanted them to like me.

This time, I'll tread with <u>caution</u>, switch on just the right amount of charm. It's a performance, not unlike what I do on my Melody Morris channel.

I have to get it right, because let's face it, starting a new school in the middle of Year 6 is not ideal.

Before long we'll all be going to secondary school, and that's major. I need to make friends now, friends I can rely on for later.

<u>Caution</u> is care that you take to avoid a risk, difficulty or mistakes.

On Monday morning, Dad drives us to Thornton-on-Sea Primary. Dino goes into class, and Dad and I go to the head teacher Ms Kowalski's office. Ms Kowalski promises that she'll give me all the support I need to settle in and make friends.

'I'm told you're a very creative girl,' she says. 'Creativity is an <u>integral</u> part of school life here. Mr Murray, your class teacher, is our music and drama expert. I'm sure you'll get along. We're putting on a fabulous school play this year. I do hope you'll audition, Melody!'

'Oh, I definitely will!'

Dad waves me goodbye and Ms Kowalski takes me along to class. Mr Murray is all smiles when I walk in the room, and while he tells everyone to make me feel welcome, I look around.

I spot Dino, sitting alone in a corner.

An <u>integral</u> part of something is a very important part that makes it complete.

My eyes surf past a sea of friendly faces, settling at last on a confident-looking girl with her hair in long plaits. Definitely one of the popular kids.

She's gazing at me with a puzzled expression, trying to work out where she knows me from. I've seen people give me this look before, of course.

I bet she follows my channel.

When Mr Murray tells the class my name is Melody Morris, the girl's eyes open wide. I turn on my most dazzling smile. When he asks for a volunteer to buddy up and help me through my first week, her hand shoots up.

'Ah, Nina!' beams Mr Murray. 'I'm sure you two will get along!'

I'm sure we will, too.

I slip into a seat beside Nina Reddy. All morning we whisper together as we work through a maths worksheet.

'Are you really Melanie Morris's daughter?' she wants to know. 'My mum loved her! She said it was just tragic, what happened.'

I smile sadly, but there'll be no tears today. My true feelings are locked safely away inside.

'I follow your channel,' Nina says. 'I never thought I'd get to meet you in real life!'

'I'm just an ordinary girl,' I tell her, but Nina won't have it. She tells me that she classifies me as a famous influencer: anything but ordinary. That makes me smile.

'Well, it's true I'm trying to rise *above* the ordinary. I aim to find the sparkle in life and share it with my followers,' I admit. 'I'm looking for the *extra*ordinary.'

Nina says, 'Wow!'

By lunchtime, Nina and I are good friends. I've promised she can be in one

---

To classify someone or something is to say what kind of person or thing they are, or which group they belong to.

of my videos. I've promised she can have the fluffy hat with animal ears from yesterday's post. I've even invited her to my 11th birthday party, which right now only exists as a vague idea in my head.

'I'm having a red carpet theme,' I tell her. I'm making it up as I go along, but Nina

and her friends are grinning at me. 'You know, like the one all the big stars walk on as they go into fancy award ceremonies! Well, we're all stars, aren't we?'

Nina's friends, Kiran, Tash and Jojo, say it sounds like the best party ever. I wonder briefly how they'll all fit into Sylvie's house and where on earth I'll find a red carpet, but these are details for later.

Nina puts her arm around me and we head to the hall for our lunch. Kiran, Tash and Jojo follow. Kiran is a funny, confident boy, who wraps his hair neatly in a patka and loves graphic novels. Tash has fair hair and freckles. She's sweet and kind and scarily good at maths. Jojo has long hair. She tells me she's going to be a scientist when she grows up and save the world from global warming.

A few hours into my first day, I have a new best friend and a very cool group of friends. Not bad work. We take our trays, piled with quiche and salad, and sit at a big centre table.

'Are you trying out for the school play?' Nina wants to know. 'I'm going for the lead role ... I LOVE singing. It's my dream career!'

At my old school I had special lessons with a voice coach. Singing is not my strong point. But this is just a part in a small-town primary school play. How hard can it be?

Nina is <u>unaware</u> that Ms Kowalski asked me to audition specially. I'm sure the head teacher has already decided the leading role is mine, what with all my media experience. I decide not to mention it to Nina.

My new best friend spears a slice of cucumber with her fork. 'So ... you've moved here because your dad is marrying

If you are <u>unaware</u> of something, you do not know about it.

Dino's mum?' she asks. 'Aww ... that's so romantic!'

I shrug. 'It'll be a small wedding, not like when Dad married Mum and it got in all the magazines! Still, any excuse for a new dress, right?'

'Obviously!' Nina says, laughing.

I spot Dino wandering past with his empty plates on a tray and wave him over. He approaches with <u>caution</u>. I don't suppose he's ever hung out with the

<u>Caution</u> is care that you take to avoid a risk, difficulty or mistakes.

cool kids at school. He was nice to me yesterday, and I'm grateful for that, so I invite him to sit with us.

I tell everyone about his mum being a would-be stand-up comedian. I explain how my dad is her manager, as well as her fiancé.

'Oh! Dino's mum might end up as famous as your mum did!' Nina says.

'I don't think so,' I snap. 'It's just a hobby, really. She works at a care home most of the time.' I smile to take the sting out of it. Nina's just trying to be nice, but Sylvie could never be like my mum, not ever. I want to steer the conversation away from whether Sylvie Owusu will ever be as famous as my mum. So I hand Dino my phone and ask him to film me. He panics and acts like I've asked him to rob a bank. Ms Kowalski did explain that phones aren't allowed in school. Filming pupils is a definite no-no, but I can't back down now.

'Don't be so boring!' I tell Dino. Instead, I switch my phone to selfie mode and start talking about school, friends and making the ordinary extraordinary.

The lunchtime helpers don't stop me, or maybe they don't see. Either way, no one intervenes.

At the end of the video, I ask my new friends to pile in and say hello.

I know I can make a great post from it. I'm going to rise above the ordinary and make the best of things, whatever it takes!

To intervene is to interrupt what is being said or done in order to stop it or affect the result.

Chapter 4

'How was school?' Dad asks later. 'Make any friends?'

I shrug. 'Loads. They all follow my channel!'

This is not exactly true, only Nina does, but the others might now. Maybe.

'Excellent!' Dad beams. 'It's great to see you settling in, Melody. We'll be happy here, I know it!'

I am about to say something, but then I remember the whole 'rise above' thing. Dad is dancing around the kitchen in an apron, pausing occasionally to stir a saucepan. The smell of bolognese sauce fills the house.

'Want to see my editing studio before we eat our dinner?' Dino asks. 'You can use it for your videos, if you like?'

'Editing studio? Sure!'

My enthusiasm fizzles out as we approach an old garage in the back yard. I wouldn't exactly <u>classify</u> it as state of the art. Even so, my eyes widen as we step inside. There are two cosy armchairs, a desk with a lamp and computer and a table with paint pots and craft materials all over it. A dozen alien puppets in various stages of completion are littered across the surface.

'My friend Abe makes them,' Dino explains. 'For the sci-fi films we make.'

'Right ...'

'Well, used to make,' Dino says. 'I've sort of grown out of it. I want to make documentaries instead, be taken seriously.'

I'm not sure I believe him one hundred percent, but I reply, 'Cool. My mum always wanted to do documentaries, but it didn't really happen.'

'Because she got ill?'

To <u>classify</u> someone or something is to say what kind of person or thing they are, or which group they belong to.

'I guess. Her fans didn't want serious stuff from her anyway. They always wanted stuff that was funny and light,' I say, sadly. 'So, does your friend Abe use this place as well?'

'Not right now,' Dino says. 'We've sort of fallen out. His mum knew that the engagement was going to happen, so Abe must have had some idea. Only he didn't tell me.'

I shrug. 'What if he didn't know?' I point out. 'It sounds to me like his mum was supposed to keep it a secret. Let's face it, Dad and Sylvie could have handled it better,' I carry on. 'But blaming your friend won't change that. It's not <u>rational</u>.'

'I suppose not,' he replies.

He fires up the computer and shows me the editing software his dad set up for him. Dino's dad lives in New Zealand since he and Sylvie got divorced.

<u>Rational</u> means reasonable or sensible.

Dino clearly misses him, but at least they can video chat when they want to. And Dino's dad clearly knows about film, because the editing software he left Dino is epic.

We upload today's video and mess about with some of the editing features.

Dad eventually pops his head in to tell us Sylvie's home from work and food is on the table. We eat spaghetti bolognese while Sylvie tells us funny stories from the care home. Some of the residents spotted her engagement ring and want to come to the wedding. I wouldn't put it past her to actually invite them.

'Will I be a bridesmaid?' I ask, twirling my spaghetti. 'I can't wait to choose a dress!'

Sylvie looks up. 'Of course you can be a bridesmaid, Melody, but it'll be a small wedding, nothing too expensive.'

I frown. 'So I have to wear jeans and a jumper to my own dad's wedding?' I huff. 'Seriously?'

Sylvie swallows. 'I'm sure we can stretch to a new dress.'

'Huh. Maybe some old lady at the care home can knit me one,' I snap, and even Dino looks shocked at that.

'Melody, apologize,' Dad growls.

'It's OK,' Sylvie intervenes.

'No, it's not,' Dad continues. 'Melody, this wedding will be the way we want it to be – small and fuss-free. And you'll just have to accept that!'

Dad hardly ever gets angry with me. Since Mum died, Dad's let me have my own way on most things. I want to argue. I want to explain that every single bit of my life has been turned upside down.

Yet I know that if I do, the hurt and sadness beneath my words will seep out. The world will see how raw I'm feeling. I can't apologize right now; I'll only end up crying.

Instead, I pick up my plate and stomp off to the kitchen. I scrape the remaining spaghetti into the food bin before dunking the plate into the washing-up bowl.

'This can't be easy for you,' Sylvie says,

To intervene is to interrupt what is being said or done in order to stop it or affect the result.

appearing in the doorway. 'Things must feel a bit <u>unpredictable</u> right now. But you seem to have done really well on your first day of school, which is a big deal. I want you to be settled and happy, Melody. And if you want a special dress for the wedding,' she adds, 'then we'll get one. We'll go shopping together next time I have a Saturday off work, OK?'

If something is <u>unpredictable</u>, it is not possible to know what will happen.

I nod, swilling my plate around
in the water.

'We'll make this work, I promise,' she
says. I wonder why she's being so kind
when I know I've been snappy and spiteful.
I wanted to hurt her, but now I'm the one
fighting back tears.

All I really want is to put my arms around
her and be comforted, even though she's
not my mum.

'I shouldn't have said those things,'
I mutter, still not meeting her gaze. It hurts
sometimes, admitting you were wrong.

'No worries,' she says. 'We'll have to get
used to each other. Learn to get along,
adapt. There'll be some blips along the
way, but whatever happens, we'll sort it
out. Trust me on that.'

I'm not sure I *can* trust Sylvie Owusu.
I hardly know her, but I have to live in the
same house with her and watch Dad acting

all mushy. They're going to get married, no matter what I say or do.

It's not ideal, but I'm stuck with it.

'Sorry,' I whisper, in the smallest voice ever.

'It's OK,' Sylvie says. 'It'll be OK.'

She opens her arms wide and I walk into them. She hugs me tight and just for a moment, I believe her.

Chapter 5

I am making a list of how to be an awesome friend.

The recurring theme of friendship is going down really well on my channel. I've even got some new followers. Fans also seem to like my new angle about looking for the best in things. I'm trying to do more of that instead of just talking about fluffy hats and sparkly headbands.

I have a new best friend. Nina is funny, talented, and kind. I have a new stepbrother who may look uncool, but is actually clever and caring. My new stepmum takes the time to make me feel welcome and wanted.

Life in Thornton-on-Sea is not as bad as I thought it would be.

I smile, adding to my list.

Something recurs when it happens again.

☆ Tell cool, funny stories to keep people interested

☆ Always have little gifts to share

☆ Have great parties and invite your classmates ☺ (ask Sylvie about red carpet party!)

What else? I show the list to Dino, who frowns.

'Friendship's not just gifts, parties and funny stories,' he tells me. 'You don't want to suggest people can buy friends!'

'*Buy* friends?' I echo. 'Don't be silly! I'd never do that!'

Just yesterday I gave everyone some little chocolate bars I'd been sent to talk about on my channel, but that's not the same thing at all.

Dino shrugs. 'Just … proceed with caution. Maybe don't try so hard,' he says.

'Don't try so hard? Seems to me like you're not trying at all,' I snap.

Caution is care that you take to avoid a risk, difficulty or mistakes.

Dino still hasn't made up with his friend Abe after their argument. Dino sits with us at lunchtime now.

I decide not to take too much notice of his friendship advice.

I head for the kitchen, where Sylvie is practising for an upcoming comedy gig. It's something about socks that vanish in the wash, but it's quite funny.

'Sylvie?' I say. 'Can I ask you something?'

'Sure!'

'When you're doing something new, it's OK to "Fake it till you make it" isn't it? That's what Mum used to say!'

Sylvie smiles. 'I think it's fine sometimes, love,' she tells me. 'Lots of people pretend to feel confident until they're more settled!'

I nod, starting to take that in.

'Sylvie ... it's my birthday in two months,' I say. 'I was wondering if I could have a party? With a red carpet theme, maybe?'

'Oh!' Sylvie says. 'Well, yes, I expect so. I'll <u>defer</u> to your dad for a final answer, but a small party sounds possible.'

'Oh, but it'll be SO cool!'

Sylvie laughs. 'I'm more jelly and ice cream than red carpet!' she says.

I immediately abandon the list of how to be an awesome friend. I start a new one, jotting down everything I need for the party. I want it to be the best party this town has ever seen.

Later in the week, Dino takes me on a guided tour of Thornton-on-Sea.

I don't find a whole lot of sparkle, but I do quite like the pier that juts out into the sea and the old-fashioned building at the end of it. Halfway along the pier, Dino treats me to an ice cream with sprinkles and strawberry sauce.

I like the sandy beach and the way the sea glints gold in the afternoon sun.

To <u>defer</u> to someone is to give way to their wishes or authority.

I like the old Victorian shopping arcade and the modern ice rink next door. I film little clips of all these things for future videos about rising above the ordinary.

I am not so keen on the boarded-up shops or the abandoned, empty buildings in the town centre though. I film short clips of rain running down a window, a broken umbrella abandoned in the gutter, smashed glass on a pavement.

I could make this town look extraordinary

49

or I could make it look grim. Film has the power to twist and tweak the truth.

I wish I had the power to twist and tweak my singing voice.

The auditions for the school play are on Friday. I have spent hours and hours practising one of the songs. I know the words inside out, but I'm not sure it sounds quite right.

I sometimes catch a glimpse of Dad's face when I'm singing, or Sylvie's, or Dino's. They don't look like they're enjoying it. Mum once said I had a nice voice ... I guess I'll just have to keep trying. Singing is an important part of the lead role.

I'll wow them eventually. I hope.

At school, things are going well with Nina and the other cool kids. I'm definitely an integral part of the gang and definitely Nina's best friend.

She's woven me a friendship bracelet

50

An integral part of something is a very important part that makes it complete.

from four different colours of thread. Next weekend I'm going ice-skating with Nina, Kiran, Tash and Jojo, and a sleepover has been mentioned, too.

'Just me and my new best friend,' she explained, and a little flame of joy crackled through me.

It's been a while since I've had proper friends. Even longer since someone wanted to be my best friend.

The only thing that makes me feel uneasy is when Nina and the others talk about the play. Everyone is convinced that Nina will be picked for the main role. There's no discussion, no anxiety, no concern that anything could possibly go wrong.

Nina's been cast in leading roles before. How will she cope when I get picked instead of her?

She has a good singing voice, that's true. Yet she must know she finally has real competition. Any <u>rational</u> person can see I'm the one with star quality. I've so much experience in front of the camera. Acting – or playing a part, at any rate – runs in my blood. She must know that, this time, she's going to miss out.

Ms Kowalski practically promised me that part on my first day. The daughter of Melanie Morris in the Thornton-on-Sea Primary play!

Rational means reasonable or sensible.

It's the kind of attention no head teacher could resist. She made it clear she wanted me to audition. That can only mean one thing.

I'm going to get that lead role, and my new best friend Nina might not be happy about that.

I don't say much, but I decide to buy a bar of chocolate to give to Nina on Friday. It might help cheer her up.

I pick the nicest chocolate bar I can find.

Chapter 6

Thursday night is my last chance to rehearse before the auditions. I'm still not happy with the song. I've practised so much that my throat feels scratchy and dry, which definitely isn't helping.

I call on as much energy as I can and launch into song right after dinner.

I watch the faces around the table. Sylvie looks uncomfortable. Dino is trying not to frown. Even Dad looks like he'd rather be anywhere but here.

'What d'you think?' I ask, but they stare back at me in awkward silence.

'You have a really <u>distinctive</u> voice, Melody,' Sylvie says at last.

'Thank you,' I reply.

'Well,' Sylvie says, standing up. 'I must go and get changed. I've got a comedy gig tonight. Better get a move on.

<u>Distinctive</u> means clearly different from others, and easy to recognize or notice.

Good luck for tomorrow, Melody!'

I hope she doesn't make any jokes about me.

I head to my room and recite my lines over and over until I'm exhausted. Mum always said you had to put the work in if you wanted to be good at anything. I'm doing that, but I don't know if it's working.

I practise in front of Dino later. I start to sing, and he looks awkward right from the start.

'What's wrong?' I demand.

'It's better than it was,' Dino says kindly. 'You know all the words. That's something! Shall I help you run through your lines for the acting bit?'

I'm word perfect there, so much more confident. My singing isn't quite right, but my acting is good, I know it is.

Dino disagrees. 'It's a bit ... wooden,' he says. 'Put some feeling into it!'

Two spots of pink warm my cheeks. I wish I hadn't asked Dino to help. He has no idea when it comes to acting. I run through the lines again, ramping up the drama.

'Um ... so, that version was a bit over the top,' he mutters. 'Try for somewhere in the middle?'

Something inside of me snaps.

'You don't get it, do you?' I snarl. 'This is my part ... mine! I have real star quality. Stage presence. People around here just don't know talent when they see it!'

I storm off to my bedroom and slam the door so hard the whole house shakes.

I'm too upset to rehearse any more. I flick through the film clips from yesterday's tour of Thornton-on-Sea. Instead of trying to put together the cool bits, I make a little film of all the horrible bits: the rain, the discarded umbrella, the empty buildings, the broken glass. Right now, they reflect the way I feel about this dump of a town.

I put a voice recording over the top. 'Want to know the truth about my new home? Thornton-on-Sea is a crummy, crumbling town full of no-hopers. Thanks to my stupid dad, I'm stuck here with a bunch of losers. That's just my new stepfamily! Or "out-of-step family", as I like to call them. My new friends are dull and have no talent ...' I go on.

It feels good to vent my anger, say the things I can't say in real life.

I watch the video back and smile.

Revenge is sweet, but this is not the kind of video I can share on my channel. Not now, not ever – I know it would upset people.

My channel is all about friendship and fun and rising above the ordinary. This angry video has to go.

Yawning, I click the delete button. I pull on my pyjamas, drag the covers up to my chin and fall into sleep.

Chapter 7

It's a while since I've auditioned for anything. Mum was in a TV ad for washing powder once, and I had to audition for the part of her daughter. I mean, I WAS her daughter ... who else were they going to pick?

Of course, I got the role. I had to say one line and wear white leggings with muddy knees. In the end they cut my line, but still, I would <u>classify</u> that as a proper acting job. That has to count for something!

Or maybe not.

'May the best girl win,' Nina says. I try to say it back because that's what best friends do, but the words stick in my throat.

Mr Murray leads us down to the school hall where Year 5 are already waiting. The auditions begin, but I don't take much notice until it gets to the main role.

To <u>classify</u> someone or something is to say what kind of person or thing they are, or which group they belong to.

Two girls from Year 5 go first. They're all right, but then it's Nina's turn. She has a great voice, the kind that gives you shivers. I think I can still beat her at the acting bit, though.

I believe that right up until the minute she starts to act. I was <u>unaware</u> of how good she was. I'm not sure how she does it, but somehow the script comes alive. I find myself leaning forward, hanging onto her every word – it all feels so real.

She's so good that even the caretaker

If you are <u>unaware</u> of something, you do not know about it.

stops sweeping the hall to listen. I think he actually wipes a tear from his eye.

'Wow,' Kiran whispers.

My confidence unravels. I have no idea what I'm doing, no idea at all. Fake it till you make it? I'm tired of faking it.

'Melody Morris,' Mr Murray calls. I want to run away and hide, but I walk into the centre of the hall, my whole body shaking with nerves.

'Ready?' Mr Murray asks. I straighten my shoulders, take a deep breath and sing.

It's not good. I forget some of the words and have to make some up. Some of the Year 5 kids giggle, and I see Mr Murray twitch as I hit a couple of wrong notes.

By the time I get on to the acting bit, I'm struggling. What's the point? I can't compete with Nina. Out of the corner of my eye, I spot the caretaker smiling as he goes back to his sweeping.

Mr Murray holds up a hand to <u>intervene</u>.

'Thank you, Melody, you can stop there,' he says. He turns to the others. 'You've all done really well. The cast will be announced at lunchtime. Back to your classes now!'

Nina links my arm, grinning. 'That was great,' she says. 'Good luck!'

'You too,' I choke out, but my cheeks are blazing.

My audition was a mess and Nina knows it. I should be grateful she's being so kind about it. I'm clearly not as nice as Nina Reddy because I'm bubbling with anger. I know it's not <u>rational</u> but it's so unfair!

I reach into my bag for the chocolate I bought to cheer her up. Suddenly it's clear that I'm the one who'll need cheering up. Maybe I can pretend the chocolate is a congratulations gift?

To <u>intervene</u> is to interrupt what is being said or done in order to stop it or affect the result. <u>Rational</u> means reasonable or sensible.

I don't want to congratulate Nina, though. I feel sick with jealousy.

I'm quiet all through maths, making stupid mistakes because I just can't concentrate.

We're halfway through lunch when the school administrator bustles into the hall and pins the cast list to the notice board. Maybe, just maybe, there's still hope?

I hear the whoops of joy before I get anywhere near the noticeboard.

Nina has the lead role. Me? I'm in the chorus, a big group of backing singers.

I sit back down and stare at my lunch. I'm not hungry any more. I watch my new friends congratulate Nina. This is not how it's supposed to be. I'm the one with acting experience ... I was in a TV advert, after all.

I know I should say something nice, but the unfairness of it all wells up inside me like poison.

I can't be glad for Nina. I can't even pretend.

Some kids on the next table are discussing the news. 'She might be called Melody, but she can't hold a tune,' one says. They start to laugh. A few people on our table are smiling as well.

Dino, sitting beside me, is flushed with embarrassment. Then Nina shoots me a look of pity.

It's the last straw.

'This must be a joke,' I hiss. 'The whole thing. Maybe you can sing, Nina, but you do NOT have star quality, no way. Not like I do. I expect Mr Murray felt sorry for you ...'

'Melody, don't do this,' Dino mutters, tugging my sleeve, trying to intervene.

I can't stop, though. I'm hurt and angry and embarrassed. I wanted people to like me, respect me, admire me ... instead they're laughing at me.

To intervene is to interrupt what is being said or done in order to stop it or affect the result.

Words spill out of me: spiteful, mean
words. I want to stop them, but I can't.
Kiran, Tash and Jojo look shocked, then
disappointed, like they never expected I
could be so mean. I don't think I expected
it, either.

Nina listens silently until I run out
of steam.

'I think your mum was pretty cool, Melody,'
she says at last, looking straight at me.

'I thought you might be, too, but you're not. You're mean and jealous ... and fake!'

She strides out of the hall, her friends following behind.

My anger ebbs away, replaced by a dawning sense of horror at what I've just done.

I've messed up big time and lost all my new friends in one go. Except for Dino. He probably wishes he could walk away too, but he's stuck with me. He doesn't look too pleased about it.

'Melody ...' he says, and I wait for him to launch into one of his big speeches.

He doesn't, though. At that moment, Ms Kowalski walks into the hall, her face fixed into a fierce expression.

'Someone's in trouble,' Dino whispers. I go cold all over. Has Nina told Ms Kowalski about what I said already? She can't have.

The whole hall is silent, watching, as Ms Kowalski turns her icy glare on me.

'Melody Morris!' she barks. 'Come to my office, now!'

Chapter 8

I blink and Dino has to <u>intervene</u>. He gently shakes my arm, which makes me move.

I'm trembling as I get to my feet and follow Ms Kowalski.

What have I done? Is it because I was mean to Nina? I don't think she'd tell on me. Nina is a nicer person than I am … I know that already.

I frown. If it's not that, then what?

I have plenty of time to think as I sit alone on a chair outside Ms Kowalski's office. The more I think, the sadder I get.

I am a terrible person. For all my videos about friendship, I'm not much of a friend to anyone.

A big tear spills down my cheek. I wipe it away with my sleeve before the school administrator can see.

To <u>intervene</u> is to interrupt what is being said or done in order to stop it or affect the result.

Eventually, Dad appears. He marches along the corridor towards me with a face like thunder. This is serious.

Ms Kowalski calls us into her office.

'As I said on the phone, we take these matters very seriously.' She's talking to Dad, not to me. 'Mobile phones must be locked away during school, for one thing. To then find out from an angry parent that Melody has made a hateful video about

our town and the pupils at this school and posted it on her channel ... it's upsetting and very concerning.'

'I've seen the latest post,' Dad says, grimly. 'I watched it right after you called me.'

The video I made about Thornton-on-Sea? It was petty and spiteful. But I deleted it ... didn't I?

My face flushes bright red. I was tired last night. Tired, stressed, and angry. What if I pressed the wrong button? Made the video live instead of deleting it?

'I don't understand!' I argue. 'I made a video, but only because I was upset. I deleted it! I definitely didn't set it to go live!'

'I'm afraid you did.'

Dad shows me a screenshot. It's there on my channel, complete with hundreds of thumbs-down emojis.

I feel sick. My whole channel is
falling apart.

'I didn't mean it! I don't really think those
things. I definitely didn't mean to post it!
I meant to delete it ... I was sure I had ...
but I was tired. It was a horrible mistake ...
it won't happen again!'

'It won't,' Dad says crisply. 'I've taken
it down. I've taken down your whole
channel ... for good. I'm not sure what
I was thinking, giving you free rein on
social media. I take the blame for this,
Ms Kowalski, but it will not happen again.
You have my word on that.'

Ms Kowalski looks at me, hard and long.
'Not the best of starts, Melody,' she says.
'We have to be very careful of the things
we say and do online. It's certainly not the
best place to get angry. Still, as your dad
has taken down the channel and is taking
this seriously, we won't punish you further.'

'Go home now and think long and hard about the effect that video may have had on everyone,' she continues. 'I'd like to think that you'll decide that a long break from being an online star is in order.'

'But ... I can't just disappear! I have thousands of followers!'

'Yes, and I'm sure none of them were impressed with that post,' Dad says. 'We'll talk later, but one thing is for sure. That was your last post, Melody Morris.'

We walk to the car in silence. I've never seen Dad this cross before.

'What were you thinking?' he growls as we drive away. 'You must have known that post would upset people!'

'I didn't mean anyone to see it!' I wail. 'I was in a bad mood. Making that video helped me get all my horrible feelings out. I thought I'd deleted it. I was really tired ... I must have clicked the wrong button!'

'No-hopers, are we?' he snaps. 'Stupid? Losers? Sylvie's seen the video,' he carries on. 'She was crying when I left to come and collect you.'

Shame twists inside of me.

'I didn't mean it!' I protest. 'Not Sylvie! She's great, she really is. And Dino too ...'

'They've done nothing to deserve this,' Dad says. 'Sylvie's done all she can to make you feel welcome. I don't think Dino's seen it, but word will get around ...'

'Everyone will hate me,' I whisper. They already do, I realize, because I said those horrible things to Nina. 'How can I show my face at school once people hear?'

'They might not hear about it,' Dad says. 'I took the video down the moment Ms Kowalski phoned me. Your mum's login details were still stored on my laptop,' he continues. 'We might have got it down in time, but you must learn from this, Melody.'

'I will!' I promise.

'The Melody Morris channel is over,' he repeats as he drives. 'I blame myself. I should never have allowed you to go on posting after your mum died. I know she'd started it with you and I just ... I didn't have the heart to stop you.'

'I'll be careful in future, Dad, I promise ...'

'No, Melody,' he says firmly. 'I thought it would give you a focus, help you through a difficult time, but I wasn't thinking straight.

You're far too young ... it was a disaster just waiting to happen.'

He pulls up outside the house, and I shrink into my seat, miserable.

Inside, Sylvie's putting on her jacket. 'Just popping to the shops,' she says.

'I'm sorry,' I blurt out. 'I didn't mean those things I said. I really didn't!'

'We'll talk later, OK, Melody?' she says, briskly. 'I've got to go out now.'

And then she's out of the door and away. I have no idea if she forgives me for messing up or hates me for it.

Dad faces me, arms folded. He looks so disappointed. I hate myself for making him feel that way.

I turn away, eyes misted with tears.

In this family, I'm the one who's out of step.

Chapter 9

My life's a mess. Messing things up has become a <u>recurring</u> theme in my life, no matter how hard I try.

This time, I've lost my friends, my channel, and I've managed to upset my new stepfamily. Even Dad looks as if he'd like to disown me. I shut myself in my room and cry it all out. When I've run out of tears, I wrap myself in my fluffy blanket and doze.

Thornton-on-Sea was a new start. I had the chance to be part of a family again, the chance to have new friends. I even had the chance to do something more meaningful with my channel, something different.

Well, I did something different all right. Now my life as an influencer is over, and I haven't got a friend to my name.

There's a knock at the door.

Something <u>recurs</u> when it happens again.

'Go away!'

'It's me,' my stepbrother says. 'Can I come in?'

He comes in anyway and perches on the side of the bed.

'It was a mistake,' I whimper. 'I was angry. I never meant to post that video! I didn't mean the things I said!'

'Your dad told me,' Dino says.

'Come to tell me I'm mean, jealous and spiteful?' I ask. 'I know that already. Come to tell me I know nothing about friendship? Guess what? I know that, too!'

'I don't think anyone at school knows,' Dino says.

'They will, though,' I wail. 'Plus, I've also lost my channel, the chance to star in the school play ...'

'Who needs all that attention anyway?'

'I do!' I wail. 'It's all I know. I belong in front of the camera! I'm just rubbish at actual acting. And singing, clearly.

Now Dad's taken my channel down!'

Dino shrugs. 'We could do a project together,' he suggests. 'Interviews maybe?

A documentary? Instead of telling people what *you* think about stuff, you could ask what *they* think?'

The tiniest spark of hope lights up inside me. Mum always wanted to do documentaries and serious TV, but nobody wanted that from her. They always wanted light, gossipy stuff.

'Maybe,' I say, dredging up a smile from somewhere.

'That's a plan, then,' Dino says. 'First off, though, you have some apologizing to do.'

I look at the friendship bracelet Nina made me, still tied around my wrist, symbol of a friendship that was over before it even began. 'As if it's that easy!'

'Saying sorry never is,' he says with a shrug.

'Right now, there's someone I want to say sorry to ... Abe. Friends matter, Melody. Don't give up on them!'

As Dino heads off, it strikes me that my new stepbrother is probably the best friend I've had in quite a while. I ditch the blanket, wash my face and brush my hair.

Downstairs, Sylvie is sitting on the sofa, scribbling in a notebook. There's no sign of Dad or Dino.

'Are you busy?' I ask.

Sylvie looks up. 'Just a few ideas for next week's gig, but I can make time for you,' she says, closing the notebook. 'How are you feeling now?'

'Terrible!' I say. 'I'm so sorry, Sylvie. I didn't mean what I said. I think you and Dino are great, I really do! Sometimes my anger appears from nowhere, and I say things I shouldn't. I think maybe I'm a bad person. I mess everything up!'

'You are not a bad person,' Sylvie says firmly. 'Not even slightly. A little bit unpredictable and mixed up, maybe ...'

If a person is unpredictable, it is not possible to know what they will do.

I sigh. 'Just a bit.'

Sylvie smiles. 'I used to get cross with Dino's dad, before we split up. I said things I didn't mean, too. These days I try to turn that stuff into humour. Making people laugh is a lot more satisfying!'

'Maybe I should try that?' I say.

'There are other ways,' she says. 'You could count to ten. Take time away from whatever's upsetting you. Do something relaxing. Think about puppies and fluffy kittens ...'

I smile. 'All at once?'

'The thing is, Melody, I think you're feeling unsure of yourself at the moment,' Sylvie says. 'No wonder. You've moved house, moved town, moved school ... you have a new stepmum and a stepbrother to get used to, new friends to make. It's a lot to take on at once,' she goes on.

'Yeah,' I agree. 'I tried so hard! I thought that if I got the lead role in the play, they'd see I was actually good at something. Now they think I'm mean and spiteful. They won't want to be friends with me any more.'

'You've certainly stirred things up a bit,' Sylvie says. 'Perhaps if you stopped trying so hard to win everyone over by showing off, they'd be able to see the real you. Honestly, Melody, it's possible for people to like you for YOU, not because of how many followers you have.'

I want to argue, explain that it's not easy being the daughter of a famous star. People expect me to behave in a certain way.

'Well, I'm clearly rubbish anyway,' I say softly. 'Dino wants me to make a documentary with him, but I'm not sure I'd be any good ...'

'I didn't know much about stand-up comedy when I started,' Sylvie tells me. 'I got booed a lot when I first started out, but I stuck with it. It takes time and practice to get really good at something. It's like everything, Melody, you have to take it step by step!'

I smile, grabbing onto the hope of that.

'Are you going to put me in your comedy routine?' I ask. 'You know, talking about your moody stepdaughter ...'

'I'd never do that,' Sylvie promises.

'There's nothing funny about how you're feeling. How about we do that shopping trip tomorrow and pick you a dress for the wedding? Does that sound OK?'

'OK!'

She moves over on the sofa and pats the seat beside her. 'Shall we find a movie? Something silly and fun? Or maybe *Star Trek* ... that's Dino's favourite!'

I sit down beside her, snuggling in the way I used to do with Mum.

Chapter 10

The trouble with being myself is that I'm not exactly sure who that is. Sylvie says not to worry because nobody really does at the age of ten. I've got a lot of growing to do.

'I used to reinvent myself every other week when I was young,' Sylvie tells me, and that makes me feel much better.

We go on our shopping trip and Sylvie buys me a blue dress and a pair of blue trainers. We get some new trainers for Dino, too.

I watch another *Star Trek* episode, this time with Dino. He shows me a channel that runs the original series on a loop. Soon, I'm hooked.

Sci-fi ... me? Who knew?

Going back to school on Monday will be the worst bit. I've written a letter of apology to Ms Kowalski to explain that I'm

really sorry for what happened. I promise
that my channel will stay down.

Apologizing to Nina is a whole lot harder.

I wait until break time and manage
to catch her as she heads out to the
playground.

'Nina? Can I talk to you?' I ask. I can see
Kiran, Tash and Jojo squaring up as if to
protect Nina from me. They probably think
I'll flip out again and start yelling.

Nina tells her friends to go on ahead, folds her arms and turns to me.

'What do you want, Melody?'

'To say sorry,' I say.

We walk to the shelter in the playing field and perch side by side on the seat.

'I was so, so out of order,' I say. 'The things I said to you. I was disappointed that I messed up my audition. Then someone made a joke about me not being able to sing, even though I'm called Melody. I felt like everyone was laughing at me. It made me mean.'

'Just a bit,' Nina says.

'I'm so embarrassed,' I tell her. 'I said some awful things. Sometimes my temper gets the better of me, but ... well, I didn't mean any of it. Your audition was brilliant, Nina. You totally deserve that part.'

'OK,' she says. 'Thank you.'

'If I could put it right, I would,' I say.

'I'd give anything to wipe it all away, start over.'

Nina shrugs. 'I said some mean stuff too, I suppose.'

'I deserved it,' I admit. 'You didn't. I'm sorry, Nina. I wish we could be friends, but I ruined all that, I know.'

'Maybe we can still be friends,' she says. My heart leaps briefly. 'I can't manage that ice rink trip or the sleepover right now, though. Then I'll be busy with stuff for the play, and it just feels a bit … well, soon.'

'It's OK,' I say. 'We'll <u>defer</u>. Put it on hold. Maybe another time.'

As Nina walks away, I remember something. Out of my coat pocket I take the forgotten chocolate bar from Friday.

'Nina?' I call. 'I got you this. To say well done on getting the part. The best girl won. And I forgot to give it to you …'

To <u>defer</u> something is to put it off until later.

Nina takes the chocolate bar. As she does, her eyes skim the friendship bracelet still knotted around my wrist. Will she ask for it back?

She doesn't.

She takes the chocolate, and for the first time a real smile warms her face.

At the end of the week, after loads of planning, Dino and I get ready to shoot our documentary at the care home where Sylvie works. I'm supposed to interview a lady called Marie, who came from Jamaica to live in Britain when she was just a child. My job is to ask her questions about her life. Dino's job is to film the interview, and edit it into a documentary. Dino's friend Abe has also been roped in to help. They've patched things up and I'm glad. It gives me hope that I can do the same with Nina, in time.

I feel like I'm on a film set when I see
the lamps Abe has set up. What if I mess
up again and make a fool of myself?

Marie appears, a tiny woman dressed up

in her best cardigan. I soon forget
my nerves and focus on the questions.
I barely notice when Dino moves in with
the camera or Abe adjusts the lighting,
because Marie's story is so awesome.

'As I came off the ship, it was snowing,'
she tells me. 'I was six years old and I'd
never seen snow before! I felt like I'd
stepped into a storybook!'

I ask Marie about how her parents came
to live in Thornton-on-Sea, how she settled
in, how she trained as a midwife.

'I met my Charley at a dance down at the
Pier Ballroom,' she tells me. 'There was
never anyone else for me, after that. We
married and had three daughters. I have
five grandchildren now!'

When the interview is over, Marie pulls
me in for a big hug. Dino catches that on
film as well. 'Amazing,' he tells me. 'You'll
have your own TV chat show one day,

I'm sure of it!'

That puts a smile on my face.

While Dino and Abe pack away the equipment, I chat to the other residents. There's Stan, who used to be a postman, and Edie, who was a scientist. Denny once toured the world playing trumpet in a band. He says he still plays the trumpet in his dreams.

When Dad sees the footage, he's impressed. He says he'll see if we can enter it into some young film-maker competition he's heard about.

The weeks slip by. Dad and Sylvie get married. The wedding goes smoothly, with me in my blue dress and trainers: Dino in his favourite jeans. Some of the care home residents come along, Stan and Marie and Edie and Denny, which makes me smile. After the registry office bit, we eat ice cream and take selfies on the pier.

Then there's a party at the Beach Cafe.

It's fun. We're officially a stepfamily now, and the 'step' jokes flow thick and fast.

Next comes the school play. I decided not to sing in the chorus after all, so I'm helping Dino and Abe behind the scenes. Painting scenery and fixing costumes is actually brilliant. Who knew?

Nina is fantastic, of course. She gets her picture in the local paper. There are three encores before the audience let the cast leave the stage, and I am right there cheering Nina on.

Do I wish it was me? Only a tiny bit, and only for a moment.

My friend Nina, the star of the show – she deserves her moment in the spotlight.

And then, at last, my birthday rolls around. Eleven. I wonder if it's the same as ten, or if by eleven you finally learn who you are?

I have no clue. I told Sylvie I'd changed my mind about the red carpet party. In the end I ask Nina and a few others to an afternoon at the ice rink.

We whirl round and round to the music and none of us are very good, so we slither and slip and fall over in a heap. It turns out that falling over on the ice is a million times more fun than you'd think. I have never laughed so much in my life. Nobody wants to go home.

'Let's sort that sleepover soon, shall we?' Nina says, when her parents come to collect her. I hug her goodbye.

'How's it going, step-sis?' Dino asks. 'Did you have a good birthday?'

'It was a great day,' I grin. 'We're getting there, aren't we Dino?'

'We are,' he says. 'Step by step, we really are.'